CROSSROADS - ACROSS TIMES

Tom Heneghan

Printing

Heneghan Printers
135A Richmond Rd
Fairview
Dublin 3
01 8371683

ISBN: 978-0-9539613-2-0

Published 2013 By: Tom Heneghan
Mobile: 087 7737729
Email: tomhany@yahoo.co.uk

CONTENTS

THE GATHERING

In my last two books I started locally and then branched out to the rest of the World.
I even went to the Moon in one chapter, and I might revisit it; we'll see.
There are things I learned about our locality I would never have known if I did not start writing.
There's history in far-off Lands, but there's history also on our local twisty boreens.
"At the end of all our wanderings, we return to the place of our very beginnings, and see it, as if for the first time": (T.S.Elliot).
Far-off lands have come back into the picture now again with the recession.
The new destination seems to be Australia, and the plane has replaced the ship.
The world seems a small place nowadays though and no place is too far away.
Travelling round the Globe is often the modern person's way of life.
More above the clouds than below them but we must always land somewhere.
Over fifty years ago many young men of 20 took the 'boat' across the water to England.
For some it was a stepping stone to a new life, but others got 'trapped'.
One hundred years ago it was the ship to America; even whole families at times.
To places like Philadelphia, New York and the windy city of Chicago.

It was a big jump from the Irish countryside to the hustle and bustle of U.S. cities.
From hilly green fields and wild flowers to sky-scraper buildings.
From meeting the bicycle on dusty roads to swarms of model-T cars.
Of course every generation has its own challenges to face and negotiate.
Our history seems to have periods of staying at home and periods of leaving.
I suppose we have to be somewhere in the world, so we try to bloom where we are planted.
This year (2013) is the year of 'The Gathering' when the diaspora return 'home'.
To be escorted in Brendan's coach on nostalgic trips through the 'old sod'.
To breathe and feel again the sights they once knew, or maybe just heard about.
They will probably see a different Land to the one their ancestors left.
But somebody said the more things change the more they stay the same; maybe.
This idea of 'The Gathering' seems a good one, so let's hope it brings abundance.
So Life goes on and the world goes round, and where we are may not be where we'll be.
And to know where we are going it's good to know where we have come from.

……………………………………

We say our goodbyes now we depart
Deep sad pain way down in the heart
We can't take it, tears start to flow
Will we ever return, to lovely Mayo

The shore in the distance, we out at sea
Our relatives waving faintly we see
We strain every muscle to get a last glimpse
Of Family and Ireland, our sadness immense

Some day we'll return to our green misty Land
To see where we came from and give it a hand
We'll all pull together in its hour of need
The 'Gathering' is here let's sow a new seed

……………………………………………………

MY OWN MEMORIES

THE TITANIC

Leaving Ireland in the olden days, for far-off shores, was by large ship.
For reasons that everybody knows the most famous of those ships is 'The Titanic'.
As I write it's the centenary year of her very first voyage; and sadly her last.
Very few drama's if any, fact or fiction, match the drama of the Titanic.
It took over two years for her construction, and over two hours for her destruction.
Only one-ninth of an iceberg is over the surface, so there is a huge mountain below.
The Titanic was the 'unsinkable' ship, on her maiden voyage, but it sank.
It was to be Captain Edward Smyth's final voyage before retirement; and it was.
Some believed that his was the powerful voice from the cold sea.
Before perishing he shouted: "All right Boys, good luck and God bless you".
1,490 people lost their lives on that April night of 1912; their earthly dreams over.
712 were rescued, amongst them was the 'unsinkable Molly Brown'.
In the midst of the mayhem the Band played 'Nearer my God to Thee'.
The Bands fiddle was discovered recently in an attic; an interesting find.

The Titanic is at the bottom of the sea for 100 years now, but it's never forgotten.
In 1985 the wreck was discovered two and a half miles below the surface.
The ship weighed 45,000 tons gross and three million rivets were used in her construction.
Lahardane in Mayo (Addergoole Parish) is now known as 'The Titanic Village'.
This Parish had 14 of her people on board as the ship sailed to her tragic end.
Eleven died and what stories the three survivors had to tell, if they could, back home.
The Timoney bell tolls in Lahardanes St Patricks Church every anniversary.
At the exact time of her sinking the name of each local person is called out.
The saddest family tragedy must be that of Athlone widow Margaret Rice.
She and her five young sons, the oldest being 10, all lost their lives that night.
The last Irish survivor, Ellen Shine, died in New York at the age of 101 in 1993.
The last overall survivor was Milvina Dean who died on 31st May in 2009.
She was also the youngest survivor, two months, on the night of the tragedy.
There is a lot written about, and talked about, the Titanic in this centenary year.
But few would ever again say a ship, or anything in this life, is unsinkable.

THE CHRISTMAS STOCKING

I spotted a Christmas stocking in the shop window in Belcarra after Mass.
There was no price on it so I ventured in through the crowd to investigate.
In the 1950's Heneghans shop was always crowded after Sunday Mass.
Dora Parkinson's cooking of breakfast wafting from the inner kitchen.
There was standing room only as I weaved my small self up to the front.
The Lady inside spotted my nose peeping over the counter and said: 'Next'.
"How much is that Christmas Stocking in the window?" I asked.
"A half-crown", she said; let's say five euro in today's money for clarity.
"I'll give you a euro now", says I, "and I'll give you the rest again."
She stared at me and suddenly the shop seemed to go quiet and everybody stared at me.
We were all frozen in time and everybody waited for my next move.
Like those westerns where a lone cowboy enters and the tavern goes 'pen-drop' quiet.
The next move was critical, and everybody knew I had to make it.
I reversed and made myself lost in the crowd, and escaped out the door.

Phew! I gave one last glance at the window and 'my' Christmas Stocking.
I went home and hung up my old sock by the fireside and hoped for the best.
We dream of big things, but often the small ordinary things make us happier.
Joy is the greatest Christmas gift but children, young and old, like to see things.
There is no specific written history of how the Christmas Stocking began.
A popular legend is that the wife of a Nobleman died and he was penniless.
He had three daughters but he had no money to pay a dowry for their marriages.
St Nicholas heard of his problem but knew that the nobleman would not accept charity.
This Saint of course has long been associated with Santa Clause.
St Nicholas was born in Turkey, but tradition has it that he is buried in Ireland.
Anyway being a man of tact as well as generousity he thought of a plan.
In the dead of night he sneaked down the chimney with three sacks of gold coins.
He noticed that the daughters had their stockings hung up to dry by the fireside.
So St Nicholas filled up each sock with the coins, and the daughters were happily married.
I might add that I am still waiting for my sock to be filled with gold coins.
"Now where did I put that old sock".

MARY MURPHY

MY OWN MEMORIES

SILENT HOLY NIGHT

Almost two hundred years ago the Austrian village of Obendorf was cut off by snow.
Just the same the villagers were cheerfully preparing for Christmas.
The school-master, Franz Gruber, was also Church organist and was practising for Mass.
Imagine his sadness when the organ, the only one in the village, broke down.
"What are we going to do now", he sighed, for music was at the heart of their festivities.
So he went to the Priest, Joseph Mohr, and suggested he write a hymn.
"A simple one as we will have to sing it without any preparation, and no organ".
Well the old Priest searched in his heart for words to best express the meaning of Christmas.
In the evening he went to the school-masters house with the lovely words of 'Silent Night'.
That night they composed their little melody to fit the words of this simple hymn.
On Christmas morning in the year 1818 this beautiful carol was sung for the first time.
And the words: 'Silent Night, Holy Night' sounded pure and clear in the Bavarian air.
The people of Obendorf being totally oblivious to the musical ripples they were creating.
Before long this simple Carol spread across the whole wide world.

On now to the equally famous and equally beautiful Christmas carol 'O Holy Night'.
This carol was written in France on a dusty, bumpy coach trip to Paris.
The Parish Priest asked the Mayor of Roquemaure to write a poem for Christmas Mass.
This sounds similar to the silent night story, but in reverse order.
The Mayor, Placide Cappeau, had written some poetry, but this was different.
Anyway he set about his task while on a business trip to the Capital City.
Thoughts of being present in Bethlehem on that blessed night inspired him.
Surprised by his own words he decided this poem should be a hymn.
So he went to his friend, Adolphe Charles Adams, and asked him to compose the music.
'Cantique de Noel' was completed to the satisfaction of Priest, Poet and composer.
It was sung for the first time in Roquemaure, France, at Christmas Eve Mass in 1847.
The best known English translation being 'O Holy Night' by John Sullivan Dwight.
I can never decide which of the these two Christmas Carols I like the best.
'Silent Night' is beautiful in its simplicity, and 'O Holy Night' is a masterpiece.
Both Carols are sung in all corners of the Earth when people celebrate the Birth of Our Lord.

....

Snow flakes falling from above
Snowdrops push up from below
Whitest whiteness all around
On roof, on tree, on frosty ground

Robin hopping light and free
Blackbird watching from the tree
On this crisp and snowy morn
Peeping sun to make it warm

Snug inside the children see
Awesome wonders by the tree
Frosty window sneaking bright
After silent holy night

....

MY OWN MEMORIES

GHOSTS OF BALLINAFAD

We had an open day at Ballinafad College for past pupils and friends.
Open days are a normal feature of Colleges, but this one was different.
Ballinafad had been closed for over 30 years and nobody knew what to expect.
I did not attend this college myself but two of my brothers did so.
I do recall though attending some plays there in a wonderful Hall.
So I wanted to bring that hall to life again, and remember it as it was.
We drove up the back avenue, not the longer front one we were used to.
There stood the College on the hill with the raised up entrance that we all knew so well.
Inside would be different though as the years took their toll without life.
The Chapel, a more recent construction, is in very good condition.
Beautiful stained glass windows intact, and the marble Altar and rails.
We enter the long corridor and view each room along the nostalgic way.
Each past pupil had their own nook and corner to linger and ponder on.
Somebody showed me the room where Micháel Cuffe practised his guitar.

I spotted a stairway and memories of my few visits started to emerge.
Sure enough at the top of the stairs stood this large wonderful hall.
Badly in need of repair of course, but I could see a play being performed in my minds eye.
The applause of the crowd and Fr Grace telling us a cup of tea and a biscuit awaited us.
Just across the way stands the magnificent refectory where we used to have a chat with the tea.
I had forgotten about the refectory, but it's just as impressive as the hall.
It's like an old banqueting room, and seems to be the best preserved place of the College.
The word sadness was used amongst the past pupils at the present condition of the place.
At Mass afterwards in Mayo-Abbey Fr Austin Fergus resembled it to the Titanic.
The similarities were striking, and both started their journeys a hundred years ago.
I am sure that a lot of boarding schools around the country have ended like this.
But it's nice to go back and recall the life and times of other days.
Some students from Ballinafad College have ended up on Missionary work in Africa.
From the misty boggy fields of Ballinafad to the hot deserts of other Lands.
That's a story for another day as we bid farewell to Ballinafad College for now.

THROUGH GEATA NA GCORP

My memory of 'Clogher House' as a child is of no house but lots of trees.
Going to school in Clogher we heard that there was a large house in there somewhere.
It had been the home of a Minister for Justice, James Fitzgerald-Kenny.
Anyway the great trees were just as interesting as the house, forming a wonderful wood.
When we left school and then returned we could see the house but no trees.
The Timber Merchant had swung his axe and the mighty oak came tumbling down.
The forlorn house and avenue were not the same without the shelter of a tree.
Is an avenue an avenue without a tree? Yes, strictly speaking, but not really.
Other such abandoned houses in the area, like Moore Hall, still have the beauty of trees.
Anyway we must move on, so they tell us, so I'll head for Drum.
Right across the road from the one-time wood stands Geata na Gcorp (Gate of the Corpse)
In olden times coffins were carried to the graveyard on men's shoulders.
It was rested on a stile, or hole in the wall, and then pushed through.
It was then carried again on the old road or path to its final destination of Drum.

Locals have restored the stile to the shape of a coffin, so it's a sight worth looking into.
I have never walked this old path to the graveyard, but there's no time like the present.
Having trod the nostalgic path I now find myself on the picturesque hilltop cemetery of Drum.
To the west we look down on Newtown village, and the restored forge.
Further on in the distance are the Partry mountains, and lovely Croagh Patrick.
To the east we see what little is left of the corn mill, and surrounding houses.
The corn mill created an industrial area round it and was booming in the 19th century.
There is a stillness here now as distinct from the busy times of the past.
Goldsmiths 'Deserted Village' comes to mind, and the similarities are striking:
"The never-failing brook – the busy mill, The decent Church that topt the neighbouring hill".
It is believed locally that St Patrick built the first Church at Drum.
The ruins of an old Church are still evident, and was in use up to the 1800's.
This hilltop Church was the seat of Drum Parish in by-gone days.
The hill is a place of great archaeological and also historical interest.
Anyway, who knows, a tranquil Chapel may again spring up on Drum Hill.

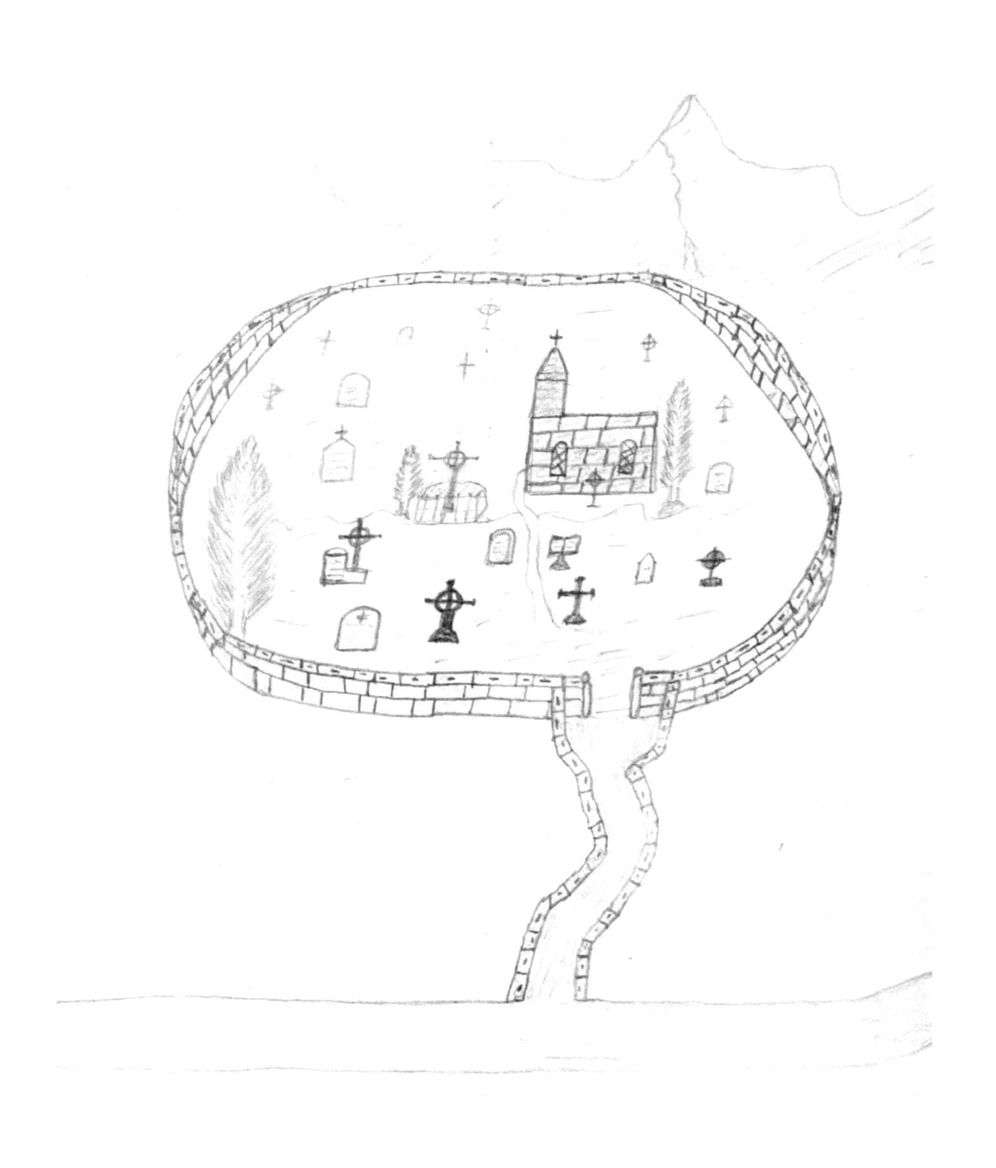

MY OWN MEMORIES

I had heard of the wonderful name Dereen-daf-Derg on a number of occasions.
I had a feeling it was in Mayo alright but what part of the County I wondered.
Imagine my surprise when I discovered it was only seven miles from my home place.
It's in the Ballintubber area, and it means: 'Little Wood of the Red Deer'.
It's sheltered by the partry mountains, and I doubt if I have heard of a better place name.
Mention Ballintubber and one automatically thinks of the famous Abbey.
As I wrote about that in my first book all I'll say is: '2016 will be its 800th anniversary'.
Ballintubber is just after winning it's first senior county football final.
To add a bit more flavour to the subject it is also their centenary year (2010).
The clubs of north Mayo seemed to have a monopoly on the Moclair cup in recent years.
Ballintubber thought centenary year would be a good time to break the monopoly.
The Ladies of the Parish, Carnacon Club, had already blazed a trail.
They have won four 'All-Irelands' in a decade, and are still going strong.
Most recent being on the 25th anniversary of the club; founded by Jimmy Corbett in 1987.

The Carnacon Ladies wear the Mayo colours, green and red, and there's a good reason.
The colours originated within the Parish, Towerhill, way back in 1885.
Here the first Gaelic Football match in Mayo was played: Towerhill V Belcarra.
There were four Ballintubber players on that historic team of long ago.
That started the ball rolling and led finally to their big day at McHale Park, Castlebar.
Their manager, James Horan, has now gone on to lead the Mayo County senior team.
Long before I heard of Ballintubber football I had heard of, and knew, Tom Carty.
As a youngster I often accompanied my Father in the van on his trips west.
More often than not we'd branch into Carty's Store, and the place was alive.
A shop, a garage, a fair canteen, even a cinema, and now the Costcutter Stores today.
I never heard Tom's famous words from the stand: "Face the Ball Ballintubber".
I can however hear them in my mind, and they must have made a difference.
His words still hang in the air on match days in the fields of Ballintubber and Clogher.
A century is a long time to wait for a County Title, but it's the playing that matters.
Baile an Tobair, village of the well, and there is no sign of it running dry.

TRAVELLING LIGHT

Whenever nowadays we see an odd round, green Caravan we remember:
A time when Travellers might call for a grain of tae, and mend a bucket in return.
The green caravan passed slowly onwards pulled by the faithful horse.
On their way to the next stop with not many cars to disturb them.
I remember them staying for a time near Clogher school and Kilboyne bog.
The holiday-makers of today have to contend with cars, cars and more cars.
From far-off lands do they realize the connection they are making with the past.
It's almost unnatural to travel by horse and caravan on the roads of today.
The caravan was a kind of 'permanent' moving home for the Travellers.
They were very handy, making amongst other things tin-can and saucepans.
If there was a hole in the bucket they mended that, and many buckets there were then.
They were also very good with horses, knowing how to heal sores etc.
The most famous of the Travellers in our area was a man called Owen Maughan.
He was a great man for a chat as he checked to see if we needed anything mended.

Tragedy struck one night when the Travellers van was struck by a train.
Owen's wife and three friends were killed at a railway crossing.
A sad ending, they passed away while travelling; remember them.
We are all travellers in one sense or another until we reach our final destination.
Actually it may be more natural to be a traveller, as we have no permanent home here.
Martin Collins tells us not to paint all Travellers with the one brush.
Just as we should not paint all Irish people, or any Nationality, with the one brush.
We are all unique souls travelling in a body, through a strange Land, for a fraction of Eternity.
Next time you meet a struggling body try and speak to the soul within.
Some believe the origin of The Traveller goes back to the great Famine of 1847.
Others claim they are descendants of the 17th century war dispossessed.
While some again state their origin goes back long before that, even to the 5th century.
Travellers have their own language which they have managed to preserve over the years.
They are a people with a unique and often turbulent history, but they have survived.
Diversity of living, and travelling light, helps us not to get trapped in security.

CARS

There were cars before Ford and the Model-T, but the T started the revolution.
The car invention turned the world upside down, or at least rushed things up.
Like the computer nowadays almost every household had to have one.
Henry Ford mass produced the car in the USA and 'everybody' had one.
My Fathers first car was a 'Baby Austin' and Christy Gilligan gave him his first lesson.
Memories of getting cars started in the morning are fresh in my mind.
The starting handle was swung many times in the frost and snow.
If that failed a pan of coals from the grate was placed in the engine to warm it up.
After that a push may even be needed but somehow we always got it moving.
Along the roadside then we'd pass a few cars broken down, just punctures mainly.
John Dunlop from Scotland was still perfecting his tyres and tubes.
Another Scotsman John Macadam was creating better roads to move on.
Moving on again and nowadays maybe you can start the car before you leave the house.
I heard that a certain car can now drive itself, so it might even go to work for us

The first car that I can trace was built by Frenchman Etienne Lenoir in 1860.
Gottlieb Daimler, from Germany, built the first commercially viable car in 1889.
I suppose Ireland can lay claim to some of the American Ford car.
Henry Ford set up the 'Ford Motor Company' in Dearborn in 1903.
His Grandfather left Ireland for America during the famine years in 1847.
By 1930 there were 15 million 'Ford Model T' sold, so things were moving.
There are now over a hundred makes of car, and the models go into the thousands.
The traffic-jam, by the way, was manufactured in the second half of the 1900's.
Everybody has their own favourite car, but the price dictates what you can own.
My Mother used to say: "as long as the car goes that is all that matters".
Lucy, the local donkey, must have mixed feelings as she peers over the wall.
The four wheel vehicles flying by have saved her a lot of hard labour.
On the other hand they have made her redundant with no two-wheeled cart to pull.
Horse-power engines there are on the roads but no horse; or humble donkey.
Ah well, not to worry, there will always be green grass to chew and tourists to view

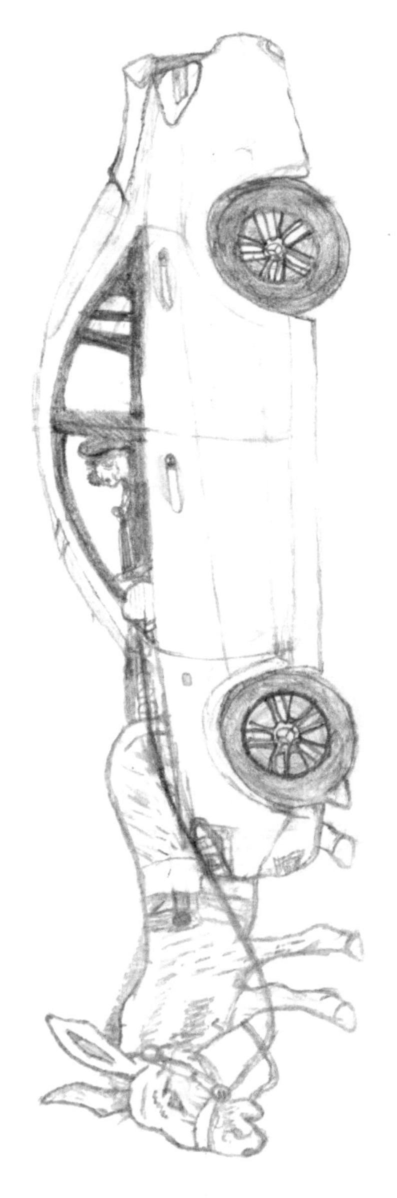
GABRIEL GRIGORE

MY OWN MEMORIES

"Msgr Horan, what exactly is going on here", asked RTE reporter Jim Fahy.
"What do you think is going on, we're building an airport", answered the Monsignor.
"Are you being absolutely serious about all this", enquired flabbergasted Jim.
"There's another load coming, I think it's marvelous, don't you?", said Msgr Horan.
So began the saga of the airport on the 'foggy, boggy hill' near Knock.
It had begun before that of course, but now Jim Fahy was to give it world-wide attention.
Msgr Horan had already built a Basilica, but would an airport to be a runway too far.
He had transformed the village of Knock saying he was 'an old man in a hurry'.
27 people owned the boggy hill, tranquilly cutting their turf year after year.
The closest they had ever come to an aeroplane was to see a moving speck overhead.
The only thing they saw soaring into the sky was the singing lark.
The only smells here came from the bog heather and wild flowers.
The only sounds here were the corn-crake, cuckoo and the whistling neighbour.
All that natural tranquillity was to be replaced with modern sight and sound.

There were reports of a white elephant roaming here, but I think it was just a giraffe.
The bog owners gave up their bog slots when the Monsignor had a word with them.
He had influence that others had not, and they knew he was not doing this for himself.
He had shown them a bigger picture and they were happy to be in it.
My Father had a story about how Msgr Horan had discovered this hill:
One day the Monsignor saw two goats passing through the village of Knock.
He inquired where they had come from, and was told from the Barnalyra, Barnacuige area.
He said he wanted to see that place, and the rest is history as they say.
Once the airport was completed his job was done and he did not live long after that.
Some said it couldn't be done, but he said 'yes it could'; risk there was of course.
One would have expected Msgr Horan to pass away in the Apparition village of Knock.
But God chose another Apparition village, Lourdes, for his final breath.
As I write it's the 100th anniversary of his birth at Tooreen, Partry Co Mayo.
Amazingly his was the first coffin into this now famous 'Ireland West Airport Knock'.
Msgr. Horan is laid to rest beside the wonderful Basilica at Knock.

BISHOP IN OUR MIDST

A Bishop must come from somewhere, but when he is from 'just down the road' it's interesting.
James from Carrajames, or Seamus Cunningham as we used to call him.
I'm not sure if a Bishop ever came from within the Parish of Balla-Belcarra before.
None recently anyway, and I'd safely say he is the first from Carrajames.
My first memory of Seamus was in Clogher school where he came to study for awhile.
That memory is vague but the next one is as clear as if it were yesterday.
Fr Seamus had just been ordained a Priest, and came to celebrate his first Mass in Belcarra.
He looked rather shy as he approached the Altar, and we hushed in our seats.
But then he astounded us with his gift of speech as we hung on his every word.
In the same decade we had the wonderful speeches of Martin L King and John F Kennedy.
Fr Seamus was not far behind, and he being still a young man in his 20's.
The actual words I remember most though were the words of our curate Fr William Walsh.
He said Fr Seamus might be a Bishop some day yet, prophetic words indeed.
Sadly Fr Walsh was to pass-away just months before he became Bishop, but I think he knew.

Anyway Fr Seamus then went his way, to England, and we went our way.
After a lot of water under the bridge he then became Bishop of Hexham and Newcastle.
My memory of Newcastle would be of Alan Shearer scoring great goals.
Maybe of more importance would be the Coal-mine and Ship-building industries.
Walking along the North Sea coast I'm sure Seamus often asks himself: "Why me Lord".
Even if it's not very clear the answer is quite simple: "Why not me".
We never know where we will end up in life, or what we will be doing.
Somebody said: "If you want to make God laugh just tell him your plans".
Interestingly he is not the first James Cunningham to be Bishop of Hexham and Newcastle.
Another Bishop of the same name served there from 1958 to 1974.
Anyway Seamus came back to celebrate Mass for us, in Belcarra, as Bishop.
After 50 years we heard that great voice again, and Fr Walsh's prediction had come true.
He says that when the time comes he will retire back amongst us.
Back to the village of Belcarra, and to the brown earth of Carrajames.
So we might have a Bishop serving us in Belcarra, unless he has to go to Rome.

I'M GLAD YOU CAME

The words kept going around in my head for a few days afterwards.
'I'm Glad You Came' is the title of a modern day song from 'The Wanted'.
So it was unusual then to hear it for the first time in a graveyard at a funeral.
Out of the blue I sometimes find myself singing those four words.
It got me thinking of all the times we said: "I'm glad you came".
Or vice versa others said to us: "Thanks for calling now, come again".
There may be times of course when we would prefer people not to call.
In general though we are happy with a visit as it often changes the atmosphere.
I saw an unattended open door recently and it felt so homely and welcoming.
It brought back memories of a different time, not so long ago at all.
The open door is saying: "Come in you are welcome, I'm glad you came".
We are living in a different type of world nowadays of course.
Doors are only opened to get out and we close them just as fast behind us.
Jesus is always standing at the door knocking, we should be glad he came.

When in a poetic mood a boy wrote to his girlfriend the following words:
"I'd climb the highest mountain for you, and swim the largest ocean for you.
"I'd go without food for days and sleep for nights just to make you happy.
"I'd travel through a wild-animal inhabited forest to reach you", 'Lovingly Yours, John'.
P.S. "I'll be over to see you on Saturday evening if it's not raining".
So it's often the small things that let us down, and we don't come when we should.
When there's a big challenge the adrenalin starts to flow and we rise to the occasion.
The small ever-day things are important too though, and it's often what makes us.
Jesus said: "I came that you may have Life and have it to the full".
We also could work wonders if we came at the right time, or even came atall.
Nowadays we send texts or emails instead of coming along ourselves.
It's better than nothing I suppose, but the presence of a person makes all the difference.
"Come to me all you who labour and are heavily burdened, and I will give you rest".
Life consists of comings and goings, and it's part of the flow of life.
Young Michelle wanted us to know she was glad we came to her funeral in Guesdian.
I'm glad I came.

It seems my Life is ended
Before it has begun
But one day lived in gladness
Is worth one hundred and one

Time on earth is over
After night the day
Did my best to be a friend
To all who passed my way

People crave a long life
Why I cannot see
When out beyond the horizon
A new life waits for me

MY OWN MEMORIES

FOXFORD WOOLEN MILLS

There were great men, and heroic women, in the history of mankind.
They did of course need the co-operation of others, but they led the way.
One such woman might be Mother Agnes Morrogh-Bernard of Foxford.
Like a lot of places in Ireland in the 19th century Foxford needed an Industry.
Mother Agnes looked around and wondered what she could do to help the area.
She saw a wonderful river, Moy of the salmon, flowing through the town.
Rivers were great sources of power then, and many a wheel they turned.
A feature of the Moy at Foxford is the way the water is shredded by rocks.
Mother Agnes saw hilly fields with grazing sheep, and the herding farmers.
"That's it", she said to herself and others, "I'll set up a woollen Mills".
"You'll do what", said some with raised eyebrows, "here in Foxford" etc, etc.
A few sceptics we need, but it's amazing how things are around us if we want to start something
Anyway the Foxford Woollen Mills were opened in 1892 and grew from there.
There were setbacks, and in 1908 the mill burned down to the ground.

But it rose again, and in 1996 a surprised 100,000th visitor was welcomed.
Today we have a thriving mill with master crafts-people using their skills.
The Visitors Centre keeps the visitor captivated as they browse in comfort.
Foxford is synonymous with tweeds, rugs and blankets worldwide.
MotherAgnes was born in England, of Cork descent, on 24th February 1842.
She joined the Irish Sisters of Charity in 1863 when she was 21 years of age.
This order was established by Mary Aikenhead, in 1815, to help the needy.
Mother Agnes set up a new Convent in Foxford in 1890, and a school followed.
In 1897 she set up a Brass and reed band, which is still going strong 100 years later.
So when you sow a seed some amazing things can happen in time.
Foxford is situated in a nice scenic area with Nephin mountain in the background.
Tranquil Loch Conn is just back the tree-covered road at Pontoon.
Up the road we have Straide; birthplace of Michael Davitt of the Land League.
Down the road we have the Rosery Priest's 'Fr Peyton Centre' at Attymass.
Foxford itself is the birthplace of William Brown; founder of the Argentinian Navy

THE FAIR DAY

Passing the outskirts of Balla recently I saw what looked like an airport runway.
I discovered it was just a large road leading into the local Cattle Mart.
It's a far cry from the Fairs on the streets of Balla, and other places around the country.
I have memories of Fairs in Castlebar where Martin Ruane might have a calfeen for sale.
The Fair took place right outside Martin's front door, so there was no 'rush'.
We had our moving Fair of Donamona, which started in one place and finished in another.
Maybe the only moving Fair in Ireland, and it was one of the largest way back.
Any occasion that gave you a free day from school, as the Fair did, was a great occasion.
The town of Balla became the countryside whenever a fair was held.
An early rise as the cattle had to be walked for miles through the dark night.
The singing of birds gave way to the lowing cattle as dawn approached on the Loona road.
Calves and bonaves (bonhams) were brought in carts, vans and small pick-up trucks.
The Jobbers arrived in large trucks and they usually stayed overnight.
The wide street of Balla was not wide enough on a Fair day in May.

A hard clap of hand on hand took place as a deal was being done over a sale.
"Here so I'll tell ya what I'll do, and this is my last bid, take it or lave it".
It was emigration then for some of the cattle as they boarded the train at Balla Station.
Geese and turkeys were sold at the 'Margadh Mor'; Fair before Christmas.
Dealers sold tools, clothes and dillisc and the canteen sold sandwiches.
Most farmers took a pinch of dillisc as they passed by, I think it was chewed only.
There was a big clean-up the day after, and the 'smell of the Fair' stayed for a week.
It was a great business occasion as people of town and country came together.
I was transported back in time recently as I took a strole through Ballinasloe Horse Fair.
This is an event that every Irish and Foreign person should experience.
The runway into Balla Mart is now the way, and there will be other ways.
The town needs the country and the country needs the town though.
Even that might change with so much imported food and modern methods.
The more 'man' goes away from nature, the more he goes away from himself.
Anyway we still have lots of green fields in Ireland, and luscious grass for the animals.

SCULPTURE BY: RORY BRESLIN

MY OWN MEMORIES

RAFTERY

Taoiseach Brian Cowan's last words in the Dail were from the poet Raftery:
"Now with the springtime the day will be stretching, when Brid's day has gone I'll run up my sail".
He used the Irish language, as did Raftery, and the original is in the next chapter.
Incoming Taoiseach, Enda Kenny, finished Brian Cowan's Raftery verse:
"Since this notion I've taken I'll never be resting, till I've made my safe way back to Mayo".
Just to cap it all Raftery's poems were published by a future President, Douglas Hyde, in 1903.
It's not clear if Raftery ever fulfilled his wish to return to his native Mayo.
In the same poem he said he'd stop off for a drink in Balla on his way to his roots.
Anthony Raftery was born in Killeaden, outside Kiltimagh, Mayo around 1780.
He became blind as a child with smallpox, but made use of his gifts just the same.
As each spring arrived he sensed and felt the growth of his native place.
The Flora and fauna of the Killeaden district were calling him home.
Green woody fields with blackberry and raspberry bushes, and wild flowers.
The winding roads to Bohola and Kilkelly just a few miles below.

He was exiled in Co Galway, and it would be just as fast to get from London nowadays.
Not that there was much difference between Mayo and Galway for this wandering poet.
I decided I should pay a visit to those two counties to get a feeling for the poetry of Raftery.
So here I am at the iron gate with 'Killedan House' carved out in big letters.
Inside is the nostalgic flora surrounded by a tranquil, bird whistling, wood.
No sign of the fauna, but one can see them grazing in the minds eye.
You can see and feel why he wanted to return to the place of his childhood and youth.
Raftery was also a fiddler and spent most of his time around the Loughrea district.
He died in this area of his adopted Co Galway on Christmas night in 1835.
Buried by the light of a candle which stayed alight in the strong wind.
So now I find myself travelling through Craughwell to find his burial place.
I pass the Turlough, largest in Europe, and reach the ancient graveyard of Killeeneen.
Buried beside the ruins of the old Church, the poet brothers Callanan are also here.
The beautiful garden across the wall would be poetry in itself for Anthony Raftery.
In my last book I promised to have one full chapter in Irish; coming up.

CONTAE MHUIGH EO

"Anois teacht an earraigh beid an lá dul cun sineadh, is tar éis na féile Bríde ardochaidh me mo sheol.
"Ó chuir me im cheann é ní stopfaidh me choiche, go seasfa' me thios I lár Chontae Mhaigh Eo".
Tá an vearsa thuas don file Raifteiri, as Cill Aodhain, in aiche Coillte Magh, a bhi breith aige.
An teideal de dán lán is ea 'Contae Mhaigh Eo', agus ta cuinhne cumha ann.
Tá Raifteiri an File is mo do Mhuigheo agus bheidir, ina dhia Yeats, de Iarthar.
I mo leabhar deireanach duairt me go bheidh caibidil as gaeilge insun leabhar seo.
Seo é anois, agus ta dochasach orm go bhuil tuiscint ag an leithoir.
Tá a lán ait stairiúil sa Contae Mhaigh Eo, agus ar fud na Tíre freisin.
Tá an Gaeltacht sa Tuir-Mhic-Eadhaigh, agus poca ait beag eile insun Contae.
Tá an Gaeilge leath morbh, ach ni bheidh Bas ag an teanga go deo.
Duairt Tomas Davis mar a leanas: "An Tír gan teanga is ea Tír gan ainm".
Tá na dhá oilithreacht lathair is mo sa Mhuigheo: Croagh Phadraig agus Cnoc Mhuire.
Deapaim a lán daoine Croagh Phadraig speisialtacht ag an Domhnach deireanach de Iúil.
Agus speisialtacht an seachtanna deireanach Lúnasa tháinig na daoine go dtí Cnoc Mhuire.

Neifin is ainm ar an Sliabh is mo do Mhuigheo, in aice Cros-mo-lína atá ann.
La Baile Mór priomhceann sa Contae is ea Caisleán-a-Bharraigh.
Sa Cluain Cearban, ag breathnu dtreo na farraige, tá an Oilean Clar
Tá Cluain Cearban an tús do Conna Mara pictiúrtha, atá sa Contae na Gaillimh.
Tógadh an Mainistir Baile-an-Tobair sa 13ú céad; 800 bhlian fadó.
Taobh isteach ta a lan cuimhne anseo insun Mainistir Baile-an-Tobair.
Loch Measca is an loch is mo sa Contae, in aice Tuir-Mhic-Eadhaigh atá ann.
Tą loch mór eile sa contae freisin is ea 'Conn', loch go han suaimhneach atá ann.
An abhainn is mór-le-rá abhainn Moy, téim isteach sa farraige in aice Beal-an-atha.
Talamh don 'seamróg agus fraoch' is ainm atha ar Mhuigheo go minic.
Tá an dath glas agus dearg ar an Foireann Liathroid de Contae Mhuigheo.
Tógainn Mhuigheo an Corn go dti an Contae trí bliann; 1936, 1950 agus 1951.
Tógainn na Mna an Corn go dti an Contae tri bliana freisin; 1999, 2000 agus 2002.
Anois tá an caibidil deireah, agus tá mé cinnte go bhuil botuin ann.
Slán anois, agus beidhmid ar ais go minic go dti Contae Mhuigheo.

MARY MURPHY

MY OWN MEMORIES

COUNTY FINGAL

How many counties in Ireland, 32 they say but now there's Co Fingal too; 33 sounds good.
If you draw a straight line from Mayo, west to east, you land in Fingal.
From the Atlantic Ocean to the Irish Sea, and Fingals motto is: 'Rich in Land and Sea'.
It is all that indeed with crops of wheat, oats, barley, cabbage, potatoes and flowers.
It reminds me of my young days in the west as Paddy and Jimmy Deacy set the oats.
First tuning green and then a golden crop swaying in the wind ready for harvest.
A lot of that has disappeared now in the west, but it's nice to see it here in the east.
Dutch and Belgian growers came to this area too and began to cultivate tulips and daffodils.
To go with the Dutch feeling there's even Windmills in the town of Skerries.
Fingal derives its name from The Danes 'The Tribe of the Fair Haired Foreigner' (Fine Gall).
It lost its 'independence' for awhile until in 1994 the County of Fingal was 'reborn'.
It's the fastest growing county in Ireland, so an All-Ireland might not be far away.
Swords is the Capital dividing in a sense, or uniting, the rural and the urban.
Some miles out is Balbriggan which is the fastest growing town in the fastest growing county.

Fingal has a wonderful breath-taking coastline drive all the way to Howth.
Out in the rich sea, apart from the fish, there's the Island of Rock-a-bill.
Here you will find the largest colony of Rossett Tern bird in Europe.
The Island of Lambay had a shipping tragedy in 1854 when 'The Tayleur' hit rocks and sank.
This merchant ship was travelling from Liverpool to Australia; 350 people were drowned.
I never knew where Loughshinny was until I ran into it on my way to lovely old-style Rush.
100 years ago Harry Hawker crash-landed his plane at Loughshinny Harbour.
He ran an aircraft company and was to die in a later plane crash in 1921.
St Patrick landed off Fingal and, it is said, carried the 'Staff of Jesus' to Ballyboughal.
The Irish name of this village being 'Baile Bachaille' meaning 'Staff (of Jesus)'.
Dublin Airport is in Fingal, and the past and future mingled together here for awhile.
A peninsula of land with a little farmhouse stood defiantly between the runways.
It would eventually be swallowed up of course, but it was an interesting sight.
Finally I take a trip to Fingal Cemetery to pray at the grave of a class-mate; Mike Ruane.
We soldiered together at Clogher School in the west, in the by-gone days of youth.

BALBRIGGAN

Drinking cappucino on the hill opposite the neat graveyard seemed strange.
The green Clonard hill overlooking the town had not changed for centuries.
Then the Millfield Shopping Centre sprung up and the hill would never be the same.
The one thing that stands out for me in Balbriggan though is the Railway Station.
If there is a more convenient station in all of Ireland I would like to see it.
You just step off the train and find yourself right in the town centre.
Across the tracks on the other side is the beautiful secluded beach.
So while waiting for your train you have a wonderful view all around.
Braemore Castle to the north, and waves crashing against the Cardy Rocks.
Behind them, in the hazy distance, the mountains of Mourne sweep down to the sea.
The Lighthouse in front looks down upon the golden strand, the sea going with the tide.
To the south of the station stands the harbour with its multi-colourful anchored boats.
This harbour was commissioned around 1765 and the town grew from it.
It's now a quiet picturesque view, but it was once a hive of activity.

Exporting ships meeting the importing ones left the harbour humming.
The fishing boats are still going out, of course, and coming in with the catch.
Beside the harbour towers the railway viaduct with its eleven arches.
Underneath streams the Beacon river, through the park, into the sea.
Overhead the Dublin-Belfast train rambles, or roars, to its destination.
Behind that, on the hill to the south, is the slender spire of St George's Church.
Nearby by is 'Sunshine House' where children shine with delight for awhile.
On to the square with the Library, Courthouse and Bracken Court Hotel.
Right in front of the Station is the old Smyco factory with all its hosiery history.
The word 'Balbriggans', meaning stockings, became famous world-wide.
Close by to the north again stands Loreto Convent and Secondary School.
The chorus of over 1000 girls voices now wafting through the air.
Replacing, in a sense, the beautiful chorus of many Nuns chanting evening prayer.
So Balbriggan railway station is surrounded by history, beauty and mystery.
At the end of the day however it's the friendly people that 'make' this 'Town of little Hills'.

BALBRIGGAN HARBOUR

MY OWN MEMORIES

LORETO WAVE

I sometimes sit on the wall, with my thoughts,
waiting for my niece.
A new wing, Gracefield House, has just sprung up
recently in front of me.
Parents wait in strategic positions for the Loreto
school exit of their Teens.
A trickle of convent girls emerge chatting about the
events of the school day.
Then suddenly a giant wave of teenage female
humanity sweeps over us.
It's a lovely sight and sound, and it makes us feel
young again.
This sight and sound happens in towns all over
Ireland, but this is the largest school.
The wave passes and its back to a trickle where my
niece and friends usually stream out.
Somebody said there is no adolescence, only just
childhood and adulthood.
I have my doubts about that, and there is definitely
teenagers in between.
Can you imagine going to bed as a child and next
morning waking up an adult; no.
A lot of these Loreto girls started their junior school
at St Peter and Pauls.
Then on to the higher classes at St Molaga's and now
'Loreto Balbriggan'.
Girls float in also from Gormanstown, The Naul,
Balrothery, Rush, Lusk, Skerries.

The Loreto wave was created by Mary Ward when she cast a stone and started a ripple.
This happened in the 17th century when she founded 'The Institute of the Blessed Virgin Mary'.
Mary Ward was English and in her lifetime schools were established all over Europe.
So whatever we do in life could have an effect for centuries to come.
The Irish branch of the Institute was established by Dubliner Frances Ball in 1821.
In fact it was in Ireland that the Order became known as Loreto Sisters.
'Loreto' being a place in Italy where it's said that the Holy Family Home was transported to.
This Loreto secondary school in Balbriggan was established in 1857.
Now over 1000 students pass through its doors daily, so life lives here.
The Mary Ward ethos of values, vision, and joy are the foundation stones of this school.
I sense a lot of joy oozing out of these Teens as they pass along the way.
Like all Human Beings they have their individual problems and sufferings of course.
Parents feel part of the Loreto experience too with gigs, musicals and rememberances.
'Loreto Balbriggan' is really a home away from home, "don't you agree girls".
Inscribed words on the entrance stone reads: "Be seekers of the truth and doers of justice".

....

What will these school Teens be
Walking light and free
The future seems far away
Not to be thought of today

Will they be doctors or nurses
Others accountants or bursars
Politicians, cleaners, teachers
Some may even be preachers

Their todays are important too
To laugh from the heart and renew
What will these school Teens be
The first thing to be is 'ME'

....

MY OWN MEMORIES

TEEN LORETO

(Sabrina Grigore)

I have had a few exciting moments so far at Loreto Balbriggan. From the day I started I had no idea what my years would be like. Lots of interesting things happen in the school buildings, but these memories are from trips outside the classroom.

One such school trip I remember was a history trip to Newgrange. It was my first trip of Loreto, and lots of new friends were made. Newgrange is the oldest buriel monument in the world, so it was great to get the chance to visit it. Luckily for us we got to go inside the tomb without feeling claustrophobic. It was so dark and even darker when the lights were switched off, having the fear that anything could pop out at anytime. The views that surrounded the tomb were magnificent. An interesting visit.

That was all for first year. One year over five to go. The second year brought a Geography Trip around the coast of Dublin. Our tour guide was strict, but funny at the same time. We looked at features of sea erosion and deposition. One such feature of erosion was a sea cliff, and one such feature of deposition was a sand spit. Lovely beaches along the way.

On to third year now, a big scary year. We take an amazing trip to Co Clare for a whole weekend I will never forget. It was the highlight of secondary school so far. The excitement of getting the day off! Our first stop towards the Burren was Bunratty Castle. Our lunch was held in the very 'luxurious'

Supermax! The queues inside were massive. Surrounding our hotel in Lisdoonvarna were green fields, and the air smelt fresh. I got to relax as I had reached my destination. I was in the west! As it was a quite time of year we had the hotel to ourselves. We were allowed to wander into our class-mates rooms which was double the fun. Next morning we had to be down at breakfast for 7 o'clock. I got up at 6 o'clock. I walked down the stairs still half asleep. At breakfast it was strange seeing the teachers on Saturday. It felt more like a weekday.

Later that morning we headed for the Burren, and to the Ailwee caves. The air in the cave was very fresh I thought, not everybody agreed. I suppose we were underground. We saw stalactites and stalagmites These resembled icicles and are formed from rainwater and calcite present in the limestone. My funny uncle says that a stalactite is a stalagmite turned upside down.

Our next destination was to the cliffs of Moher passing by Lahinch where surfing was done at the coast. It was lovely to see the cliffs as you would always see them in pictures, and here I was actually looking at them. I made sure not to fall off.

To end the day we had a disco which was a great laugh, but the next morning was departure day. It was sad to say goodbye, but we couldn't stay forever. One last smell of the fresh morning air, and the dew on the fields, and the bus left. The memories I will never forget and I hope there will be a lot more trips to come. Sabrina.

FAMILY TREE

Finding out where you came from, who were your ancestors, is big at the moment.
If you have the time and the patience it can be an interesting journey.
Especially for people whose Parents have come from different Nations.
The ancestors are not always that easy to find as vital records may be lost along the way.
Names too may be spelled differently, so there's quite a bit of work in it.
None of us will make it back to Adam and Eve, but some aim for the 15th century.
The gap is long, in time and change, from then to now but records can turn up.
I suppose the important thing is to look-after the people who are on earth with us now.
People sometimes speak of the generation gap between young and old.
The gap may be there at times but mostly I think it's a generation-bridge.
The young need the old, and vice versa, just as the earth needs the sun and the air.
The young keep the old young, and the old keep the young's feet on the ground.
The young are vibrant and lively, the old are full of wisdom and experienced.
I heard it said that when an old person dies a library closes its doors.

Some people travel thousands of miles to find their ancestral roots.
My own family roots are within a radius of ten miles going back for generations.
Great-grandparents coming from Guesdian, Monard, Welshpool, Ballyshaun, Cappavicar.
So my roots are deep into south-Mayo soil, but I'll keep digging.
Great-grandparents only go back to the 1800 or 1900's, so dig on.
Sitting in Belcarra Chapel for mid-night Mass my thoughts wandered back.
Back 100 years or more and our ancestors sat where we were now sitting.
While it's interesting maybe it's not that important to find our ancestors.
Jesus said that his family were those who did the will of his Father.
So in Heaven our earthly family may not have the same significance as here.
If you meet a long lost enemy there it will be the same as meeting a friendly relative.
So family-tree work is an earthly journey, but if we find ancestors we can pray for them.
Of more importance is to 'find' ourselves in our maze of contradictions.
Who am I, where did I come from, what am I doing, where am I going.
Incidentally my Father John was born 100 years ago (1913) as I write, so time slips by.

Life is a
mystery
Time
slips
by

MY OWN MEMORIES

POLISH WEDDING

You would not normally find me looking out a window at 4 in the morning.
It was the month of June and daytime was gradually taking over from the night.
I watched the rain falling on the green fields outside; it must be Ireland.
No, Poland actually and the long wedding was drawing to a close.
Earlier I had travelled through the Polish dawn with Leseck , his niece Caroline and Parents.
A going-away party was held for the groom at his house in the early morning.
An unusual time to have a going-away party, but that was the tradition there.
The Groom then kneels in front of his Mother and she blesses him with the crucifix.
(She repeats the exercise later by blessing the Bride with the same crucifix).
Then we all went to collect the Bride at her house; no problem of the bride not turning up.
Going-away tears flowed as a sad song was played on the accordion.
We drive to the graveyard where Bride and Groom visit their ancestors graves.
Finally we make it to the Church and the Couple become man and wife.
Hanna Jolanta Sokotowska became Mrs Jarostaw Wojno that blessed day.

On then to the reception where I add an Irish flavour with a tune on the bagpipes.
I felt like the Pied-Piper as the children followed me around the tables.
The Poles break into Sto lat, Sto lat quiet a lot during the celebrations.
It's a traditional song, meaning '100 years', wishing good health and long life.
Anyway that's how I found myself looking out a window in Poland at 4 a.m. in 1996.
It's nice to experience the traditions of other Nations, especially Poland.
More Polish people than other Nationalities arrived in Ireland during the Celtic Tiger days.
The number of Polish Nationals here could reach as high as 200,000.
Polish political parties have campaigned in Ireland during the 2007 general election.
Three voting locations had been set up at Dublin, Cork and Limerick.
Some say Poland and Ireland have similar histories, so they feel at home here I hope.
The Poles sent us a Pope earlier on in the century to clear the way for them.
The World is getting smaller by means of travel, but the population is getting larger.
The Irish went to England and America but the Poles and others came to Ireland.
'100 years, 100 years, may they live, live with us'
'Sto lat, Sto lat, niech zyje, zyje nam'.

POLSKI ŚLUB

Normalnie nie znałazlbyś mnie patrzącego przez okno o 4 nad ranem.
To był miesiąc czerwiec i dzień delikatnie zaczął przejmowac kontrole nad nocą.
Patrzyłem jak deszcz pada na zielone pola, to musi być Irlandia.
Nie, Polska tak na prawdę I długi ślub, przesuwał się ku końcowi.
Wcześniej musiałem przejechać przez Polskę z Lesieckim, i jego siostrzenica Karolina i jej rodzicami.
Pozegnalne przyjęcie dla pana młodego odbyło się w jego domu wczesnym rankiem.
Niecodzienny czas zeby mieć przyjęccie pozegnalne, ale tarnto taka tradycja.
Pan młody klęka przed swoja matka I ona świeci go krzyżem świętym.
Potem wszyscy poszliśmy odebrać pannę młoda z jej domu; nie ma problemu ze Panna młoda się nie pojawi.
Odchodząc Izy płynna, gdy smutna piosenka jest grana na akordeonie.
Jedziemy na cmentarz gdzie Pan młody I Panna młoda odwiedzaja groby swoich przodkow.
Ostatecznie przyjeżdżamy do kościoła i para zostaje mężem zona.
Hanna Jolanta Sokołowska zostaje Panią Jarosław Wojno w ten błogosławiony dzień.

A potem do recepcji gdzie dodałem Irlandzkiego smaku grając na dudach.
Czuje się ja Pied-Piper, gdy dzieci chodzą za mną dokoła stołu.
Polacy śpiewają sto lat, sto lat w czasie uroczystości
To jest tradycyjna piosenka, oznaczająca 100 lat', życząc dobrego zdrowia i długiego życia.
Tak czy inaczej tak znalazłem się patrzeć przez okno w Polsce o 4 nad ranem 1996r.
Jest milo doświadczyć tradycji innych narodowości, szczególnie Polski.
Więcej Polaków przyjechało do Irlandii niż innych narodowości w czasie panowania Celtyckiego Tygrysa.
Liczba Polaków może sięgać nawet tak duzo jak 200,000.
Polskie partie polityczne ustawiały kampanie w Irlandii w czasie generalnych wyborów w 2007r.
Trzy locale wyborcze zostały ustawione w Dublin, Cork i Limerick.
Niektórzy mowa ze Polska i Irlandia maja podobne historie, dlatego oni czują się tu jak w domu, mam taka nadzieje.
Polacy zesłali nam Papieża wcześniej w tym stuleciu żeby przetarł drogę dia nich.
Świat robi się mniejszy w znaczeniu podroży, ale ludzkość staje się większa.
Irlandczycy wyjechali do Anglii I Ameryki, ale Polacy i inne narodowości przyjechałi do Irlandii.
Sto lat, sto lat, niech żyje, zyje nam.
(Tłumaczenie: Justyna Krokowska)

MOON MOODS

It was midnight when I saw the moon peeping up behind the Church spire.
I never knew the moon would rise at midnight, but then again why not.
Usually I looked up and there was the moon, or not as the case may be.
The daily journey of the Sun is familiar, but we think the Moon is all over the place.
Then again maybe it's me that's all over the place because I haven't studied the Moon.
So I find the Moon tricky to pin down, as I don't know where or when it will appear.
On the first Sunday in Advent I spotted a new moon in the evening sky.
The faint rim is a beautiful sight to behold and even a sign of hope.
On a frosty night the stars are a heavenly sight, and fills you with wonder.
So many worlds out there in the Universe, and we think we are big sometimes.
The seven stars forming the Plough are always there, also the Milky Way and the Cluster.
Our nearest planet neighbour of course is the homely moon lighting the night sky.
I'm off now to the local strand to 'sea' what effect it has on the tides.
There are two tides daily as gravity from the Moon pulls on the water.
Large volumes of water rise and fall according to the position of the Moon.
Anyway the water is either lapping the shore or way out nearly as far as the eye can see.
The Sun also affects the tides when it's in a certain position to Moon and Earth

The Moon is about 250,000 miles away, not much when you say it fast.
It is a ball of dusty rock, and is four times smaller than the Earth.
It is full of huge craters and high mountains; mount Hadley is almost three miles high.
It has no atmosphere as we know it, no weather, no air and no blue skies.
We only ever see one side of the Moon and the far side is called, yes, 'The far Side'.
The Moon orbits the Earth while at the same time the Earth orbits the Sun.
The Sun is 400 times bigger than the Moon, but it's also 400 times further away from us
One number cancels out the other, so they look the same size from down our way.
When we gaze at the Moon it's fascinating to know that a man actually walked there.
The first man to do so, Neil Armstrong, has passed away as I write.
His co-pilot, Buzz Aldrin, says he used a pencil to get off the Moon.
When he went to press the lift-off button it was missing, so a pencil can be useful.
I suppose the Moon would be a good place to get away from it all; lonely though.
Now that Man had reached the Moon an Irishman decided to go to the Sun.
When he was told he would be burned up he said: "No problem, I will travel by night."
Oh, I have just made a discovery: the waxing moon, new moon, rises in the morning.
While the waning moon, getting smaller, rises at night, so I'm learning.
By the way, I have not seen the blue moon yet and I have seen strange things.

NATASHA BEEGAN

MY OWN MEMORIES

STRANGE HAPPENINGS

We all have memories of interesting things that have happened during our lives.
Things we love to think about and other things that make us cringe.
Some people have more dramatic ones than my few, but mine may be of interest.
I have to depend on the memory of my siblings for the first strange happening.
I was about two or three and my birthday was in full swing with cake and candles.
When it was over my mother was tiding up and she said: “Where’s the candles”?
I said calmly: “ I ate them”, and sure enough no trace of the candles could be found.
I just hope I had blown them out first, as Houdini acts at two is not advisable.
I gave up the candle diet after that as amongst other things it was expensive.
Those candles could have been put away for the next celebration, but t’was my birthday.
My next memory is of the eating variety too; a time I spent in sunny Italy.
Before I went to sleep I ate half an apple leaving the other half on my locker.
If I only knew the activity that was going on while I slept I would have had nightmares.
I turned on the light at 3 a.m. and must have jumped three feet off the bed.

The apple was covered in an army of ants, and they are larger than Irish ants.
There were thousands of them forming a line, ten deep, down the locker and out the door.
Out into the bathroom and down the drain-pipe of the shower; three stories up mind you.
I had seen them march up the side of trees before, but never inside the house.
I threw the apple into the toilet, a few killed in battle I fear, and the rest marched away.
I can't remember if I slept after that, but I never left an apple on my locker again.
A third incident is of the time I was travelling with a friend in the Wicklow mountains.
My car started to heat up as some smoke from the engine informed me.
I needed water but none in sight, and no house in sight high up there.
After about only three minutes a van appeared and two men got out.
They said little or nothing as they examined the smoking engine.
They then opened their van door and stuck a small saucepan into a barrel of water.
The engine was cooled, my problem solved, and it was all over in five minutes.
Off they went as silently as they had arrived, and we were just as silent in wonder.
They had the appearance of men, but Angels they may have been.

WATER

Anybody who lived in the countryside in by-gone days knew of the spring well.
Just a narrow deep hole in the ground, and at the bottom cool clear water.
Little steps were erected to escort you down safely with your bucket.
These wells were dotted all over the countryside, and they were natural.
A lot of them are not used nowadays as pipes and bottles take over our world.
Some Blessed Wells of course, like Tober-macduach, are beautifully restored.
I do recall as a child smiling in anticipation of a cup of spring water to stake my thirst.
Water has a gentleness all of its own, but you can't hold back flowing water.
Like the wind it navigates round you as it flows on its way to the sea.
'I bubble up from the brown earth on the high peak of Cnoc Ard.
'And come tumbling down the mountain-side', so went one of my school-day poems.
The thunder and beauty of the Niagra Falls is quite fascinating to behold.
Like an old person entering eternity a river becomes tranquil as it enters the ocean.
A world without water would be pretty dead as its uses are many and varied.

We can live much longer without food than without water I believe.
Like our bodies more than half the world is made up of water, but most of it is salty.
Actually the Oceans contain 97.5 percent of the worlds water.
That leaves just 2.5 percent of 'drinkable', but maybe we can de-salt some of the oceans.
Two million people die each year from diseases attributed to polluted water.
We very often take water for granted, so we must not abuse or waste it.
As the old saying goes: "You never miss the water till the well runs dry".
It's not a surprise to hear that water is held as Sacred by many Beliefs.
Jesus himself was baptised with water in the river Jordan by John the Baptist.
Down through the centuries the spring wells have drawn crowds for pattern days.
A tranquil stream calms us down, and a water-fall is awe inspiring.
Artists have amply captured the beauty of the stream and magnificence of the waterfall.
Even the rain, which we often complain about, is of great value to the land.
Just ask any person in hot climates where drought occurs frequently.
Or a graceful swan who glides down upon a new tranquil winter lake.

....

WATER-*FORMS*

Gentle Streams, thunderous waterfalls
Tranquil ponds, great lakes
Morning dew, hanging icicles
Spring wells, marshy woods

A little trickle, a racing river
A white cloud, a dense fog
A light drizzle, a heavy torrent
A rippling brook, a chopping sea

Light vapour, heavy rain
Dripping leaves, showers on grain
Oceans lapping, giant waves
Autumn mists, Monsoons

....

MY OWN MEMORIES

EUCHARISTIC CONGRESS

Walking in Procession of this Eucharistic Congress
revives memories of other times.
Girls in white dresses strewing flowers along the way
on Corpus Christi day.
A million people attended the final Mass of the 1932
International Eucharistic Congress.
It was the first time for the Congress in Ireland and it
united the people after an ugly civil war.
The crowd was captivated by the voice of Pope Pius
X1 relayed from Rome.
And by the rendering of Panis Angelicus by John
McCormack of Athlone.
The people spoke of the joy of the occasion for many
years afterwards; even today.
80 years later and we have the Eucharistic Congress
to give us a lift again.
There are similarities economically between 1932
and 2012 with our present recession.
The Congress may be what's needed to put our Lives
in proper perspective.
Today we have too much communication, but not
enough Communion.
The closing Mass last time was at The Phoenix Park,
this time at Croke Park.
Interestingly one of the organisers is Ger Brennan, a
member of the Dublin football team.
The Mass in this Stadium is emotional for him as he
has just won an All-Ireland here.

The Mass, Eucharist, was instituted by Jesus himself at the last supper.
It has been carried on through the ages by the Priests back to the Apostles.
Priests, and people, sometimes risking their lives to offer it on hidden Mass-Rocks.
Since his resurrection Jesus returns world-wide to earth in the Eucharist.
Eucharistic miracles there have been over the years, amongst them being the following:
A Priest had doubts about the real presence, but at the consecration the Host bled.
This miracle happened at St Christina's Church Bolsena, Italy in 1263.
As a result the feast of Corpus Christi was instituted by Pope Urban 1V.
Interestingly enough the blood type in all approved Eucharistic miracles is AB.
A more recent reported miracle is from high up in the Cantabrian mountains of Spain.
From 1961 to 1965 four young girls were having visions of Our Lady at Garabandal.
On one occasion the crowd watched in awe as the Host appeared on Conchita's tongue.
The first International Eucharistic Congress was held in Lille, France in 1881.
This present one in Ireland is the 50th, and the next will be held in The Phillippines.
Pope Benedict XV1closes the Congress, via Satellite, by showering God's blessing on us.

GOD

God is Love

MY OWN MEMORIES

ANFIELD and AINTREE

"And they're off, coming up to Beechers Brook, and everybody safely over.
"On to the next fence and Rutherford is a faller, there's a right pile-up".
I'm writing this on an April morning; Grand National Day at Aintree.
My mind wanders back 45 years to another day at the great race-track.
While Aintree is famous for this steeplechase it has made Foinavon famous also.
Even people who have little interest in horse racing remember this horse.
The year is 1967 and there was a big fall at the fence after Beechers Brook.
One after the other horse and jockey come tumbling to the ground.
Down go all the favourites, but one horse managed to weave its way through.
After avoiding the mayhem 'Foinavon' goes on to victory at 100 to 1.
He had made it into the history books and one of the fences is now called: 'The Foinavon'.
Aintree Village is just a few miles north of the 'Irish City' of Liverpool.
Even the word Aintree seems to have an Irish sound to it: 'Aon Tree'.
Local legend has it that the tree, cut down in 2004, was on Bull Bridge Lane.
The race course was built in 1829, and 'Lottery' won the first Grand National in 1839.
I wonder what excitement awaits the racing fraternity on this beautiful April morning.
Over to Anfield, "and there's a penalty, GERARD SCORES, and Liverpool lead".

From Aintree to Anfield and the memories from here are just as strong.
Both places start with the letter A, both have seven letters, and are just a few miles apart.
There is no tree in the field of dreams, but there is a lot of budding talent.
Hansen passes to Lawrenson, on to Dalglish, now to Houghton, to Keegan and he scores.
I have one memory of Irishman Steve Highway scoring a goal in a Cup Final.
Anfield Stadium was built in 1884 and, believe it or not, it was Evertons home ground.
When Everton moved out the Anfield owner, John Houlding, had a stadium but no team.
So he decided to form another football team, and Liverpool F.C. was born.
The first match in 1892, in front of 200 spectators, was against Rotherham Town.
The name Bill Shankly stands out as one of the great managers of Liverpool.
His words: "Football is not a matter of life and death, it's more important than that".
The Club Anthem is: 'You'll never walk alone' a hit song for 'Gerry and the Pacemakers'.
Actually the word Anfield comes from the townland of Annefield in New Ross.
The name was bestowed by the famous Co Wexford shipbuilder Robert Samuel Graves.
He left his native Annefield in the 1850's and later became Mayor of Liverpool.
40 per cent of the Worlds trade passed through the City's Docks at one stage.
Liverpool is the city of the Beatles, and 'yesterday' has come and gone.
Over to Aintree, "and 'Auroras Encore' wins the 2013 Grand National".

SEP-TIMBER

When my niece and nephew were small they were always fascinated by tree cutting.
Travelling from Dublin to Mayo in the autumn there were many such sights.
In a poem-like mood they sang: 'Timber, Timber', as the sawdust fell to the ground.
Followed closely by a branch of a tree as the lethal chainsaw sliced through.
I have no idea where they heard those 'Timber' words pronounced so deliberately.
The words had a great meaning for me because I love pruning trees in the autumn.
I suppose you could call it the trees annual hair-cut, and the saw-dust the dandruff.
To compare sawdust to dandruff is unfair, as sawdust gives a dry look to a soggy wet field.
The trees are shaking off their leaves with a great gusto wind or storm.
The green of the summer giving way to the reddish-brown gold of the autumn.
"I think that I shall never see, a poem as lovely as a tree": (Joyce Kilmer).
Autumn is my favourite season, even if the winter is not far behind.
Year's end is approaching, but ends always give way to new beginnings.
They say you can set a tree in any month with an R in it; they come together.

Not many speak about the winter sun, but when it appears it's great.
No matter how cold it is outside when it shines through the window it's hot.
Because it's low in the sky it shines directly through the window; just discovered that.
Make sure you sit in a room facing the south in the winter-time of year.
I suppose it's a bit like sitting in front of the fire-place in the wintry nights.
The cut autumn timber is now put to good use after years of growth.
The smell of timber and sight of the wafting smoke beckoning the neighbour to enter.
Maybe I'm thinking of a different age here, but some things never die.
Memories of our ancestors are fresh at this time, and the hearths they sat around.
The only news was the local news, and the rest of the world was out there somewhere.
Jack Tuffy quoted to me once: "You shall not know the seasons but for the leaves on the tree".
I think he was referring to the 'end times', so maybe we should keep ourselves pruned too.
In America they call autumn 'The Fall', maybe from the fall of the leaves and other things.
My Grandmother died in November, and I think it's the most natural time to die.
To be dead with the trees in the winter, and rise to blossom in the spring.

MARY MURPHY

MY OWN MEMORIES

JUDY COYNE

Judy Who? Never heard of her, and indeed her work is better known than herself.
If we look around the developments and beauty of Knock today we think of one person.
Monsignor James Horan automatically comes to mind, and rightly so.
However, long before Msgr Horan, and even after, there was Judy Coyne.
She, along with her husband Liam, set up the Knock Shrine Society in 1935.
The wonderful work of the Knock Handmaids, and Stewards, flowed from that.
The sacrifices made for the Invalids by all these Volunteers is amazing.
As children we sometimes passed Judy's tranquil residence at Bridgemount.
"Nothing much happening in there", we thought as we crossed the bridge.
But the activity sometimes reached fever pitch, and all for Knock.
Important meetings chaired, and mountains of mail to be dealt with.
Food for invalids and pilgrims was prepared in there and then brought to Knock 20 miles away.
Both Judy and Liam threw themselves totally into making Knock an international Shrine.
Care-taker Pat Bourke from Killavalla could not avoid been drawn in.

One of Judy Coyne's works stands out straight away as you enter the Church grounds.
She it was who commissioned the beautiful large statues at the Apparition gable.
They are made of Carrara Marble by the Roman sculptor Lorenzo Ferri.
That was only a tiny bit of her work, but it was an important one for her.
50 years after the 1879 Apparition Knock was almost forgotton about.
On a visit to Lourdes Judy and her husband Liam were struck by the invalids.
"Why not a place like this in Ireland", they thought, and so began their incredible Knock story.
An invitation to the Pope was the first item on Judys agenda at all Society meetings.
The Pope did come as we know, and that was one of her wonderful dreams fulfilled.
Liam, a District Court Judge, died suddenly after 20 years of this Knock work.
Judys drive up the Bridgemount tree-covered avenue was lonely after that.
She thought of quitting but another 50 years of 'labour' awaited her at Knock.
She saw in the new Millennium and died in 2001 at the age of 97.
Some of the stories of the Knock handmaids are just as heroic as her own.
Edited by Ethna Kennedy read Judy's life story in her book 'Providence my Guide'.

……………………………………..

Dark clouds roll round the sky
Pierced by brilliant light
Blazing- up Knock's hillside church
In the dark, dark night

Mary Joseph and St John
Angels hoover round
Altar holding Lamb and cross
Above the holy ground

Blessed Mayo you were chosen
To receive this vision
What a blessing what a joy
To see the Queen of Heaven

……………………………………..

MY OWN MEMORIES

HABEMUS PAPAM

The retirement of Pope Benedict XV1was an unusual event, and took the world by surprise.
It got me thinking of all the Popes during my lifetime and memories of where I was.
I used to walk on Sundays to see Pope PaulV1 giving his blessing at Castlegandolfo.
Now I did not walk all the way from Ireland, mind you, but from a town called Albano.
Albano was about five miles away, so a group of us sometimes took off on foot.
Up the big hill and past Lake Albano which is about 1000 meters deep.
Looking back now I probably did not appreciate that walk of beautiful scenery.
Anyway we arrive at Castlegandilfo and Pope Paul makes his appearance at a balcony.
He had a wonderful golden voice as he sent us on our way with a blessing.
It was at Castlegandolfo that Pope Benedict spoke his final public words: Buona Notte.
Another memory of that time would be the morning I drove a car through St Peters square.
Right up to the door of St Peters Basilica, with very few around in the still atmosphere.
A far cry from the crowd that packed the square for the white smoke of 13313.
Habemus Papam is familiar, but now we also have Papam Emeritius; retired Pope

The first Pope was Peter chosen by Jesus himself 2000 years ago.
Pius X11 was the Pope in Office the year I was born, he announced a Marian Year for 1954
That's the year all those statues of Our Lady were erected at crossroads around Ireland
Next came John XX111, 50 years ago, who was known as 'The Good Pope John'
He was followed by Pope Paul V1, and then came Pope John Paul 1.
He was Pope for just 33 days when he died, and was known as the smiling Pope.
I had the privilege of shaking hands with the next Pope, John Paul 11, in the Vatican.
He was shot in 1981, at St Peters Square, on the feast-day of Our Lady of Fatima.
Later he went to Fatima and placed the bullet in the crown of Mary's statue, there it stays.
John Paul 11 was the only Pope to visit Ireland, but we may have an Irish Pope some day.
Then came Pope Benedict XV1, he being the first Pope to retire in 700 years.
Now we have Francis from Argentina, the first Pope from the Americas.
We may have bumped into him on the street as he studied in Ireland for a time
A new Pope brings new hope, but it's ourselves that must change.
We wish him well and, as he asked, we pray God's Blessing on him. Viva il Papa.

THE COMPUTER

I'm always amused when I think of what Mike Garry wrote about the old man and his Paper.
On his way to school Mike would be given a penny to buy the newspaper.
On his way home he'd read an episode of 'Gussie Wee' before he'd deliver the Paper.
Dying to find out how Gussie Wee was getting on he'd call a few days later.
"Do you need another newspaper", says Mike. "No", replies the old man, "I'm only at page 5 yet".
You'd get the impression that is the way some people use the computer.
They'd stay on it for hours, and there's a lot more pages in there than in a newspaper.
While I don't read many newspapers I'd still prefer it to sitting in front of the computer.
It's an amazing instrument of course, and some do make great use of it.
I am sure it had something to do with getting a man on to the moon.
I make most use of the computer as a modern day typewriter; which are now obsolete.
If you leave out a word you don't have to type the sentence again like in the old days.
Just pop the word in wherever it's missing and the other words move over.
Very convenient of them, and that does save an enormous amount of time.

The first computer was built in 1945 and was the size of a large room or two.
Everything was big and heavy in those days, but things have changed rapidly.
The old telegram arrived by bicycle, now we press a button and the message is instant.
A letter took at least a week to arrive, a text takes less than a second.
The Human Being does not relax for long, always new inventions to ponder.
Someone said: 'Life is something that happens to us while we are planning something else'.
Here we sit typing, but our minds are in a different part of the world.
We are disconnected from human contact in a way our ancestors never could be.
A lot of things like banking and paying bills are done 'on line' nowadays.
Ah well, they say we must move with the times; as long as we don't move too far too fast.
Everything has it's advantages I suppose, but it's important to 'be' as well as to 'do'.
We could now reverse the old saying to: 'Don't just do something, sit there'.
Modern inventions can take control of us instead of the other way around.
In the supermarkets you are now often dealing with a computer as you pay.
It says to you "put that item in the right place", and you can't answer back.
Come –now- puter.

Any
question?

MY OWN MEMORIES

CROSSROADS ACROSS TIMES

We meet many crossroads on our journey through the rocky road of life and time.
Most may be sign posted, but others must often be agonised over.
We sometimes wonder if we had taken a different turn would life be different.
Why did we turn left instead of right or maybe go straight ahead.
Some people believe that the road is laid out for you, but it can be a foggy path at times.
Maybe we took the long way around and learned some valuable lessons.
Scott Peck talks about 'The Road Less Travelled' in his well known book.
"Three roads converged in a wood, I chose the one less travelled and that made all the difference".
Most of us follow the crowd on the wide road, not noticing the fulfilling paths.
Decisions, decisions, the gentle thief in 'Oliver' kept reviewing the situation.
He wanted to turn but the way he knew best kept him on a cul-de-sac.
A new road seemed attractive, but alas, he felt he had to think it out again.
The word decide, from the Latin, means 'to cut off from'; one road only.
Someone said that death is the easiest of journeys because you don't have to park.

Regarding the physical roads we have many types, especially nowadays.
Major highways, dual-carriage-ways, normal roads, twisty boreens and tranquil paths.
Our ancestors had no roads, but paths trodden in the forest gave them the idea.
Michael Mullen takes us on historic trips through Mayo in his book 'The Road Taken'.
The Saw-Doctors give the immigrants a nostalic journey back home on the N17.
They can feel and see again the stone walls and green fields as they travel along.
My own first road was up the boreen at Donamona, to the well with my Mother.
Then back the dusty tree-shaded road to Clogher national school.
Years later I walked the cobble-stone road, used by St Paul, on his journey out of Rome.
In between there were many minor and major crossroads to negotiate.
Not forgetting the most important road of all: 'The Road to Emmaus'.
I read an interesting book called: 'The Road to You, by Robert J Furey.
A lot of roads lead away, so a road towards ourselves could be valuable.
We meet the first major crossroads when we decide to leave the nest.
It may be just down to the local cross, but the turn we take could make all the difference.
Safe travelling.

NATASHA BEEGAN